*An Appalachian
Mother Goose*

An Appalachian
Mother Goose

JAMES STILL

ILLUSTRATIONS BY
PAUL BRETT JOHNSON

THE UNIVERSITY PRESS OF KENTUCKY

Publication of this volume was made possible in part
by grants from the E.O. Robinson Mountain Fund
and the National Endowment for the Humanities.

Editorial and Sales Offices: The University Press of Kentucky
663 South Limestone Street, Lexington, Kentucky 40508-4008

02 01 00 99 98   1 2 3 4 5

Library of Congress Cataloging-in-Publication Data
Still, James, 1906-
    An Appalachian Mother Goose / James Still : illustrations by Paul
Brett Johnson.
            p. cm.
    Summary: A compilation of Mother Goose rhymes as collected
from the Appalachian region oral tradition.
    ISBN 0-8131-2092-6 (hardcover : alk. paper)
    1. Nursery rhymes, American. 2. Children's poetry, American.
[1. Nursery rhymes. 2. Appalachian region—Poetry.] I. Johnson, Paul
Brett, ill. II. Title.
PZ8.3.s858Ap 1998
398.8'0973—dc21   98-23117

To my godsons

Jacob Alexander Hiram Bradley
Christopher Lee Thompson
Jacob Singleton
James Franklin
Evan Smith

Preface

There was a time not so long ago when the hills and hollows of Appalachia abounded in creekbed roads, and travel was by horseback, mountain sled, or shank's-mare (walking). The one-room schools were taught by masters of limited learning, and the custom was to recite lessons in a chorus of voices. Thus they were called Blab Schools. Among verses of renown, students got "by heart" the Mother Goose rhymes and often changed them to match their time and place and understanding. And sometimes they created their own.

Do not take us for a dunce
Reciting lessons all at once.

Higgledy, piggledy, my smart hen,
She lays goose eggs for gentlemen;
Gentlemen come from miles away,
To see goose eggs my hen doth lay.

Humpty Dumpty sat on a wall,
And if he'd managed not to fall,
Teeter or totter, clung to the last,
We'd had an egg to break our fast.

Miss Buxom Hubbard
Hied to her cupboard
To fetch her dog a bone;
The cupboard was stuffed
With pies, cakes and puffs,
Her flea-bitten dog got none.

Hey diddle diddle,
The cat played the fiddle,
The cow sang ballads to the moon;
The little dog laughed,
He thought them daft,
And the dish banged away with the spoon.

Little Nancy Etticoat
Had a pretty petticoat
She bought at the Isom Fair.
It was green and brown
To highlight her gown,
And with reds and blues
To flatter her shoes
And yellow to glitter her hair.

Little Nancy Etticoat
Was so proud of her petticoat
And being the center of all eyes
Her cheeks got all rosy,
She turned up her nosy,
And her head swelled to
   considerable size.

Jack was nimble,
Jack was quick,
Scorched his pants
Jumping the candlestick.

Little Bopeep has lost her sheep
And can't tell where to find them.
Leave them alone, they'll come home,
Tails full of burrs behind them.

Sing a song of six cents,
A pocket full of rye;
Four and twenty blackbirds
Baked in a pie.
"Isn't this absurd,"
Said one baked bird,
"Why didn't we up and fly?"

Lying tongue, lying head,
Here's what the preacher said:
Coming up for a liar
Is brimstone and fire.

Jack and Jill went up the hill
To fetch a bucket of water:
Jack fell down and cracked his crown,
And Jill died of laughter.

Jill came to life, became Jack's wife,
And soon they had a daughter;
Jack spent his days in several ways,
The womenfolk fetched the water.

☹

I do not like you, Doctor Pell,
The reason why I know full well;
You made me swallow a bitter pill,
Drink castor oil, cough syrup swill.
I do not like you Doctor Pell.

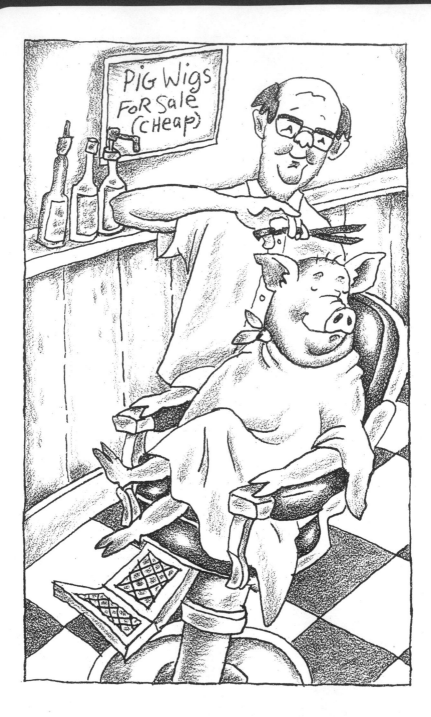

Barber, barber, shave a pig,
How many pig hairs make a wig?
Save at least twenty-three
To make a wig for baldhead me.

Winter is coming, my grippe
   I can't knock it,
Kindly drop a copper in an old-
   timer's pocket:
If you haven't got a copper, your
   warm coat will do,
If you won't part with your coat,
   ker-chew! ah, ker-chew!

---

grippe: a bad cold
copper: a penny

Baa, baa, black sheep
Have you any wool?
Yes, yes, yesterday
Three bags fulls;
They sheared me close,
The sheared me bold;
I burn in the sun,
In the shade cold.

☌

Charlie Mann,
　　Charlie Mann,
　　　　Skipped the custard,
　Ate the pan.

☾

The man in the moon came down too soon
To inquire the way to Hazard;
The man from the sun arrived too late
And got himself caught in a blizzard.

♋

Old John Bean, world's oldest man,
How come you eldest in the land?
I ate cornbread and soup beans,
Drank mountain dew in between.

John Bean, 1812-1922

Pat-a-cake, pat-a-cake, baker's man,
Mix me a stack-cake, bake it in a pan;
A slice for Mary Belle, a slice for Lum,
A slice for Sally, and save me some.

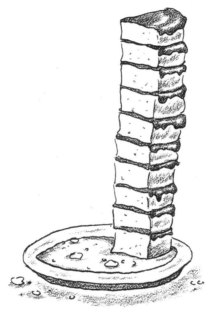

Tweedle-de-dum and Tweedle-de-dee
Shuffled up a hill to see out to sea;
They saw seven sailors sailing a canoe,
They saw seven sawfish saw it in two.

What are little boys made of?
What are little boys made of?
Stubbed toes, runny nose,
Dirty hands and torn clothes;
And that's what little boys are
        made of;
And that's what little boys are
        made of.

What are little girls made of?
What are little girls made of?
Buttons, bows, squeals and cries,
Tears and sighs and mud pies;
And that's what little girls are
        made of;
And that's what little girls are
        made of.

Raincrow, raincrow
What do you say?
I say rain
For today.
Wheelspindle, wheelspindle
Is this so?
Until it happens
We'll never know.

Rain, rain, go away
We children want to play.
Don't come Saturday,
Don't come Sunday,
Come again some school day.

---

wheelspindle: a wood thrush

Old Prentice Hogan never took a bath,
He smelled like a squirrel, both a
   squirrel and a calf;
As snakes slip their skins, ants shed
   their wings,
Old Prentice peels off pretty in the spring

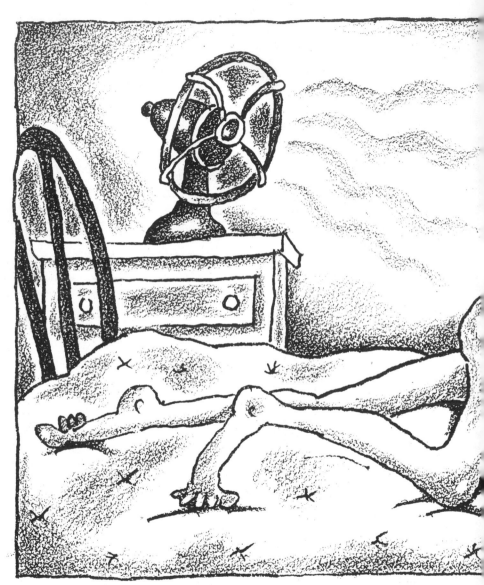

Old Boney Face loved his ease,
He'd fight for it tooth and claw,

And when the nights grew awfully hot
He slept entirely raw.

O where, O where has my little dog gone?
O where, O where can he be?
He's gone to sniff with the dog
    next door,
That's where he is, is he.

There's a tale of a cat
Who lost her tail in a spat;
But a tale of this sort
Is necessarily short.

Mary had a little Lamb,
Its fleece was white as snow,
And everywhere that Mary went
Soot was sure to snow.

It followed her to school one day,
It was against the rule,
It recited in her school one day,
Mary's lamb was nobody's fool.

Peter, Peter, pumpkin eater
Had a wife and couldn't keep her.
Now she's selling bows and bells
And now she keeps him very well.

✿

Pretty maids and homely maids
Who dread to have a speckle
Have only to bathe in honey dew
To never know a freckle.

Matthew, Mark, Luke and John
Hold my nag till I spring on;
Hold him right, hold him tight,
Or he'll kick you out of sight.

Tom, Tom, the blacksmith's son
Stole a pig, and away he run.
    Not much of a stunt,
    The pig was a runt,
Tom with a stick bore the brunt.

Big nose, red nose,
Strawberry nose,
Where did you get
Your rosy red nose?
Sunshine and moonshine,
Who-shot with turpentine
That's what gave me
A nose that glows.

Here am I
On the roof,
When I'm alone
I'm aloof.
When I'm down
and in the town
Everybody is
around.

---

who-shot: spirits

"Will you lend me your mare to ride
Across the hill to the other side?"

"She suffers with hollow tail and stifle,
And with these ills I dare not trifle."

"I'll pay you well, more than rare
To ride her to the Isom Fair."

"You've cured my horse, you full know
Money is what makes the old mare go."

---

stifle: weak knees

Rowdy, dowdy, Jitney Jones
Bought a dog with no bones;
He sold the dog to Jim Oak
Who carried the dog in a poke.

One penny's nigh none,
Two is barely some,
Three is a good many,
Four is jim-dandy,
Five will buy
A poke of candy.

●●●●●

---

poke: a sack

Susan Priggs, Susan Priggs,
Susan Priggs had a dozen wigs.
She wore them up, she wore them down
To shock the people of the town.
She wore short wigs, wore them tall,
The wig liked least was none at all.

○

Bow, wow, bow, wow!
Old dog, who's your master?
"Mean" Howard's dog
And you'd better run faster.
Bow, wow, wow!

I had a little wife the size of my thumb,
I never made her cook, set her in the sun;
Fed her bread and tiny bites of meat,
Bought birdskin shoes for her tiny feet.

Father Goose, jolly fellow,
Have you feathers for my pillow?
Certainly, tad, but ask me better,
Take a pen and write a letter.

tad (tadwhacker): a small boy

Churn dasher, churn dasher,
Won't you work a little faster?
Chad is waiting at the gate
With a steaming griddle cake;
Without butter Chad will choke,
Let's not let Chady croak
Churn dasher, churn dasher,
Won't you work a little faster?

One, two, three, four, five,
I caught a rabbit alive;
Six, seven, eight, nine, ten,
I put him in a pen.
Five, four, three, two, one,
Letting him go was half the fun.

A sharp-tack once asked me
"How many rocks in Carr Creek's bed?"
I answered wisely, I quickly said,
"As many rocks as are in your head."

Sharp-tack: a wiseacre

Ned NcNoink killed a shoat,
What he had left was not of note;
Heggy McDever got the liver,
John Felt got the melt,
Bill Lears got the ears,
Thomas Crams got the hams,
Tandy Mart got the heart,
Dee Hanks got the flanks,
Ned McNoink was left the *ooink*.

There was a cattle trader out for a buck,
When he lost his crook he had no luck.

There was a preacher shouted hill to hill,
Now that he's hushed it's echoing still.

There was a butcher who cut his thumb,
Bleeding he cried, "Fee-fie-foe-fum?"

A crow laid her eggs in a cowbird's nest,
As a cowbird builds none, tell me the rest.

There was a shoe that lost its mate,
Instead of walking it had to wait.

The stocking was hung exactly as writ,
On Santa's big foot it didn't fit.

Jack Pratt would not eat fat,
His wife would not eat lean,
If baked opossum was on the table
They both ate as long as able.

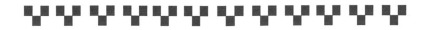

Harry Larry Pridemore Newe
Had two sweethearts, couldn't
    marry two,
One he wived, the other sent
    away,
Winks at the latter New Year's
    Day.

Diddle, diddle dumpling, my son John
Caught a catfish forty feet long;
It started at one foot, then stretched
    to forty,
The tale ended long though it started
    shorty.

George Porgy, huckleberry pie,
Winked at the girls and made them cry.
When the school came out to play
He kissed the girls and ran away.

There was this girl in Bulan Town
Who was married in a silken gown,
And then wore gingham forever after.
I speak in pity, not in laughter.

Ride a cornstalk
To the Isom Fair
To see what Tommy will buy:
A new gourd fiddle,
An old whimmy-diddle,
An apple to bake a pie.

Tadwhacker, tadwhacker you bad
    creature,
Bringing a snail to your teacher;
Tadwhacker, tadwhacker, what gave
    you he?
Twenty whacks across the knee.

---

tadwhacker: a small boy

There was a clever wife
Who lived in a shoe,
She had a pack of young'uns
And she knew what to do;
She washed them and combed them,
Picked burrs from their heads,
Gave them a sugar-tit and put
    them to bed.

Riddle, riddle, randy crow,
How many thieves do you know?
One trading cattle, one buying land,
One with a pistol in his hand.

---

sugar-tit: a lump of sugar tied in a rag

There was an old crow
  Sat dozing upon a clod;
That's the whole story,
Crow, nod, clod.

A boy is a greenhorn
   until
He has fallen out of a tree,
Seen a haint,
Stubbed off a toenail,
Eaten a green persimmon,
Been stung by a yellow jacket,
Climbed a slippery elm,
Been flogged by a gander,
Kissed a pretty girl.

Sink or swim, live or die,
The best eating is gooseberry pie;
The worse victuals are pickled beans,
Hog jowl and turnip greens.

Way down yonder in the hickory grove,
The wind did blow, chickens did crow,
Clock of heaven struck eleven.
And O! how my sore heart did ache
To see the hole my spade did make.

Grave-digging

I saw an icicle burning bright
I saw two angels in a fight
I saw a dwarf twelve feet high
I saw a giant one inch nigh
I saw a rabbit chase a dog
I saw a snail lift a log
I saw a river run up hill
I saw milk refuse to spill
I saw a thief who never steals
I saw a wagon with square wheels
I may be dreaming, it may be true
If you believe me, so are you.

Old woman, old woman,
    shall we go a-berrying?
Speak louder, kind sir,
    I'm hard of hearing.
Old woman, old woman,
    will you me marry?
Of course, kind sir,
    why do we tarry?.

Little Boy Blue, come blow your horn,
The sheep's in the meadow, cow's in the
    corn.
Is this the way you mind the cattle?
Have you no fear of switch or paddle?

Why did Ole Jerb Bowen take a bale of
    hay to bed with him?

To feed his nightmares

I saw it come on a stormy night,
I saw it come and it was white;
It was—still it wasn't—you understand!
My head was brave but my feet wouldn't
    stand.

a ghost

The frog I played with
Was the clever sort
To give me a handsome
Strawberry wart.

I bathed in May dew,
Alas and alack,
The stingy frog
Took the wart back.

☞ Bad Tommy Turner
You're due several lickings.
Whittle you a bill,
Go peck with the chickens.

Which came first
Egg or hen?
Who followed whom,
Monkey or man?

Which was first
Flowers or bees?
Why should I care
Swinging through the trees?

If a witch-broom in a tree you spy,
You're under the gaze of the Evil Eye;
Hang a horseshoe over the door,
The Eye will close forevermore.

Witch-broom: a tufted growth on a tree caused by fungi

Hickory, dickory, dock
A mouse ran up the clock
To check the time and weather;
A cat was there
High on a chair
Oiling the works with a feather.

—

B

My first word will bite you,
My second will attack you;
Put them together and you're
    imagining things.

bug-bear

I sold hen's teeth at the Isom Fair,
Had a peck of trouble coming clear.

Sold my nag on Jockey Day,
Sold him twice but he wouldn't stay.

Went to a stir-off big and bold,
Got pushed into the sorghum hole.

Preacher swore I'd go to Guinea,
In that case amongst a plenty.

Bought back my nag to cure remorse,
First time ever kissed by a horse.

Jockey Day: horse swapping on the first day of Circuit
 Court
stir-off: molasses making
sorghum hole: a hole in the ground to discard skim-
 mings
Guinea: a hot place.

Here is sulky Sue;
What shall we do?
Her lips are a sickle
Turned to a pickle.

I sold my horse, it pained my heart,
From my dear nag I could not part;
How get him back, yet save face
And salve my pride in any case?

Rue-Back

---

rue-back: to swap back even

The day it rained cats and dogs
Was the day after snowing polliwogs;
The day it poured gold—alas, I spent
Grabbling taters, didn't catch a glint;
The day it drizzled silver dollars
I was hunting ginseng up in the hollows;
The night billions of stars fell
I was underground digging a well;
The minute this world comes to an end
I believe I'll start all over again.

Mommy cooked a moonshine pie.
Did I like it? No not I.
It gave pappy a bloodshot eye.

---

taters: potatoes
grabbling: digging

The hatchet and the hammer fell out.
If the hatchet had more edge,
The hammer had more clout.
They knocked and banged in and out
Until both forgot what it was about.

J

"Nanny cat, nanny cat, where have you been?"
"I've been to the courthouse to see the judge."
"Nanny cat, nanny cat, why do you gloat?"
"I petitioned the judge to give cats the vote."

There is an old woman lives under a hill,
She fries pies, and fries them still;
She fries pies upon an open spit,
Eat too many and you're apt to split.

How much is a jillion?
A blue million.
A short quart?
A rip and a snort.
How far's "Up the road"?
Ten hops of a toad.

What's a lick and a promise?
A doubting Thomas?
A baker's dozen?
A kissing cousin?
How stack the deck
For a hug around the neck?

---

spit: a griddle

James Still

James Still was born in 1906 in Lafayette, Alabama, in a family of ten children, five boys and five girls. His early years were spent on a farm near Buffalo Wallow. Following high school, he earned degrees from Lincoln Memorial University, Vanderbilt University, and the University of Illinois. In 1931 he moved to Hindman, Kentucky, to work in community programs sponsored by the Hindman Settlement School. Since then he has called Knott County his home.

The next year he joined the staff of the Settlement. Among his duties was operation of the library. He spent one day a week delivering books on foot to schools in remote hollows. Teachers called him the "book boy." Later he supervised the bookmobile program, often serving as driver.

In 1939 he moved to a log house on Little Carr Creek between the waters of Dead Mare Branch and Wolfpen Creek. His friend Jethro Amburgey, famous dulcimer maker, willed this house to him as a lifetime inheritance. He grew most of his food, tramped the wooded mountains and high fields, and took part in the life of the isolated neighborhood. It was here that he wrote many of his poems and short stories and the award-winning novel *River of Earth*.

When he moved to Little Carr Creek he expected to stay a single summer. Fifty-four years later he still calls Wolfpen home, but for the past sixteen years he has lived on the Hindman Settlement School campus. He was drafted at age thirty-six and served in North Africa and the Middle East during World War II. He has also been away for periods of teaching and travel in

twenty-four countries. An interest in Mayan civilization resulted in fourteen winter visits to Central America. For twelve years he taught at Morehead State University.

James Still's first book of poetry, *Hounds on the Mountain*, was published in 1937; the novel *River of Earth*, in 1940. His other books include three collections of short stories: *On Troublesome Creek*, *Pattern of a Man*, and *The Run for the Elbertas*. The novel *Sporty Creek* was followed by the children's books *Way Down Yonder on Troublesome Creek*, *The Wolfpen Rusties*, *Jack and the Wonder Beans*, and *Rusties and Riddles and Gee Haw Whimmy Diddles*. Another book of poetry, *The Wolfpen Poems*, was published in 1986. His most recent book, *The Wolfpen Notebooks*, appeared in 1991. Since 1935 his poetry and fiction have appeared in the *Atlantic*, *Yale Review*, *Saturday Evening Post*, *Poetry* (Chicago), the *Virginia Quarterly Review*, *Esquire*, and other periodicals.

Numerous awards and prizes have come Still's way: the O. Henry Memorial Prize for Short Story, the American Academy of Arts and Letters Award, the Marjorie Peabody Waite Award, a Berea College Special Weatherford Award, two Guggenheim Fellowships, seven honorary degrees, and other honors. He was Kentucky's Poet Laureate from 1995 to 1997.

Paul Brett Johnson

Paul Brett Johnson is a well known artist from Kentucky's Appalachian coalfields. He was a library student of James Still during his high school days at Hindman, Kentucky. He has illustrated many children's books, including *The Cow Who Wouldn't Come Down* and *Farmers' Market*, both of which he also wrote.